W9-BQT-463

Smudge

First published in the United States, Canada, Great Britain, Australia, and
New Zealand in 1997 by North-South Books, an imprint of Nord–Süd Verlag AG,
Gossau Zürich, Switzerland.

Library of Congress Cataloging-in-Publication Data is available.
A CIP catalogue record for this book is available from The British Library.
ISBN 1-55858-788-8 (trade binding) 10 9 8 7 6 5 4 3 2
ISBN 1-55858-789-6 (library binding) 10 9 8 7 6 5 4 3 2 1
Printed in Italy

For more information about our books, and the authors and artists who create
them, visit our web site: http://www.northsouth.com

A Michael Neugebauer Book
North-South Books · New York · London

My name is Smudge, and I am black like burnt toast.

My whiskers are all tied in knots, and I sat in some chewing gum, but that doesn't matter.
I am old, and I tell stories.
And here's one now.

Long ago, before my tail became stiff like a broom handle, I was sitting in the garden drinking some warm milk that my mother had just given me.

The sunshine and the sweet smell of flowers wrapped themselves around me like a blanket. Nearby, a grasshopper sang a cradle song, and I was drowsy and happy and warm.

All of a sudden, a big bird with beady eyes swept down from the sky. Giving my ear a sharp pinch, he picked me up and flew away with me.

I hardly had time to wave good-bye to my brothers and sisters before we disappeared over the treetops.

We soon reached the bird's home, which was filled with bald-headed babies.

At first they only used me as a brush to polish their long beaks. But as time passed, I grew quite close to them. Soon I felt just like one of the family.

I quickly learned to chirp and ruffle myself up. I even thought about laying an egg. But the one thing I just could not do—no matter how hard I flapped my arms—was fly like they could.

And one day, they all flew off without me. I hardly had time to wave good-bye to my new family before they disappeared behind a cloud.

I sat in the moist grass,
wondering what
to do next.

All of a sudden, a thin dog with a wet nose ran up. Giving my tail a quick bite, he picked me up and ran away with me.

We soon reached the dog's home, which was filled with growling babies.

At first they only used me as a ball to toss around. But as time passed, I grew quite close to them. Soon I felt just like one of the family.

I quickly learned to bark and wag my tail. I even thought about burying a bone. But the one thing that I just could not do—no matter how fast I moved my legs—was run like they could.

And one day they all ran off without me. I hardly had time to wave good-bye to my new family before they disappeared over a hill.

I sat on an old log and wondered what to do.

All of a sudden, a fluffy rabbit with big ears hopped out of hole. Giving my paw a hard squeeze, he picked me up and hopped away with me.

We soon reached the rabbit's home, which was filled with powder-puff babies.

At first they only used me to plug up a hole in the wall. But as time passed, I grew quite close to them. Soon I felt just like one of the family.

I quickly learned to nibble carrots and wiggle my ears. I even thought about digging a tunnel. But the one thing that I could not do—no matter how high I jumped—was hop like they could.

And one day they all hopped off without me. I hardly had time to wave good-bye to my new family before they disappeared in the tall grass.

I sat by a blue stream and wondered what to do.

All of a sudden, a long fish with silver scales swam up. Giving my toe a quick nibble, he pulled me down and swam away with me.

We soon reached the fish's home, which was filled with slippery babies.

At first they only used me as an anchor. But as time passed, I grew quite close to them. Soon I felt just like one of the family.

I quickly learned to hold my breath and blow bubbles. I even thought about making ripples. But the one thing I just could not do—no matter how quickly I flapped my feet—was swim like they could.

And one day they all swam off without me. I hardly had time to wave good-bye to my new family before they disappeared down the stream.

I sat beneath a shady tree and wondered what to do.

All of a sudden, a grey squirrel with a bushy tail climbed down. Giving my whiskers a brisk tug, he pulled me up and scampered away with me.

We soon reached the squirrel's home, which was filled with bushy-tailed babies.

At first they only used me as a pillow. But as time passed, I grew quite close to them. Soon I felt just like one of the family.

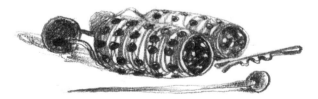

I quickly learned to hang upside down and balance on thin branches. I even thought about storing acorns. But the one thing that I just could not do—no matter how far I leaped—was jump like they could.

And one day they all jumped off without me. I hardly had time to wave good-bye to my new family before they disappeared through the leaves.

I sat in a garden and wondered what to do.

All of a sudden, a brown rat with a big smile was beside me. Giving my cheek a soft kiss, she cuddled me in her arms and carried me off.

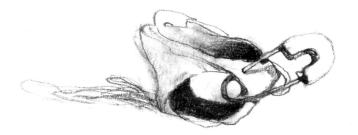

We soon reached the rat's nest, which was filled with long-tailed babies.

From the very first they didn't want to use me for anything—they just hugged and cuddled me and welcomed me home. Right away I felt close to them—just like one of the family, and of course I was, since they were my very own mother and brothers and sisters.

I already knew how to twitch my nose and squeak. I didn't even have to think about combing my whiskers. There wasn't a thing they could do that I couldn't do. For after all, I was a rat—just like them!

And I knew they would never leave me!

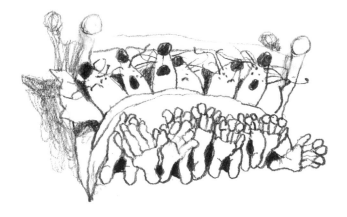